Jeremy

Pirate School

The Birthday Bash

Illustrated by Ian Cunliffe

PUFFIN BOOKS

PUFFIN BOOKS

Published by the Penguin Group
Penguin Books Ltd, 80 Strand, London WC2R 0RL, England
Penguin Group (USA) Inc., 375 Hudson Street, New York, New York 10014, USA
Penguin Group (Canada), 90 Eglinton Avenue East, Suite 700, Toronto, Ontario, Canada M4P 2Y3
(a division of Pearson Penguin Canada Inc.)
Penguin Ireland, 25 St Stephen's Green, Dublin 2, Ireland (a division of Penguin Books Ltd)
Penguin Group (Australia), 250 Camberwell Road, Camberwell, Victoria 3124, Australia
(a division of Pearson Australia Group Pty Ltd)
Penguin Books India Pvt Ltd, 11 Community Centre, Panchsheel Park, New Delhi – 110 017, India
Penguin Group (NZ), 67 Apollo Drive, Rosedale, North Shore 0632, New Zealand
(a division of Pearson New Zealand Ltd)
Penguin Books (South Africa) (Pty) Ltd, 24 Sturdee Avenue, Rosebank, Johannesburg 2196, South Africa

Penguin Books Ltd, Registered Offices: 80 Strand, London WC2R 0RL, England

puffinbooks.com

First published 2003
010 - 10

Text copyright © Jeremy Strong, 2003
Illustrations copyright © Ian Cunliffe, 2003
All rights reserved

The moral right of the author and illustrator has been asserted

Printed in Singapore by Star Standard

British Library Cataloguing in Publication Data
A CIP catalogue record for this book is available from the British Library

ISBN 978-0-141-31595-9

Patagonia Clatterbottom
is the head teacher of Pirate School.

It's her birthday …

… and Smudge, Flo, Ziggy and Corkella are

Jeremy Strong once worked in a bakery, putting the jam into three thousand doughnuts every night. Now he puts the jam in stories instead, which he finds much more exciting. At the age of three, he fell out of a first-floor bedroom window and landed on his head. His mother says that this damaged him for the rest of his life and refuses to take any responsibility. He loves writing stories because he says it is 'the only time you alone have complete control and can make anything happen'. His ambition is to make you laugh (or at least snuffle). Jeremy Strong lives near Bath with four cats and a flying cow.

Books by Jeremy Strong

GIANT JIM AND THE HURRICANE
THE INDOOR PIRATES
THE INDOOR PIRATES ON TREASURE ISLAND
MY BROTHER'S FAMOUS BOTTOM
MY DAD'S GOT AN ALLIGATOR!
MY GRANNY'S GREAT ESCAPE
MY MUM'S GOING TO EXPLODE!
THERE'S A PHARAOH IN OUR BATH!

PIRATE SCHOOL – JUST A BIT OF WIND
PIRATE SCHOOL – THE BIRTHDAY BASH
PIRATE SCHOOL – WHERE'S THAT DOG?
PIRATE SCHOOL – THE BUN GUN
PIRATE SCHOOL – A VERY FISHY BATTLE

Contents

1. Pirate School

Pirate School is run by a
nightmare on legs. Her name
is Mrs Patagonia Clatterbottom.

What a fright!
Her nose is like an
ancient potato.

Her hands
are like
snapping
lobsters.

She wears a flaming
orange wig. She
has a wooden leg
and often rides
about in a
boat-pram.

2

Most of the children are afraid of her, apart from Ziggy. He's not scared of anything, except rice pudding.

Even Miss Snitty, the school secretary, is afraid of Mrs Clatterbottom. Patagonia is always shouting at her.

"Push my boat-pram on to the deck, Snitty!"

"Get me a choccy-biccy, Snitty!"

The children are taught all the things that pirates do.

Mrs Muggwump teaches swinging on a rope, helped by her pet toucan. Mad Maggott shows them how to

walk the gangplank and Miss
Fishgripp teaches hand-to-hand
fighting. Sometimes they have to do
all three at once and that makes big
problems.

Every so often Patagonia brings a
special teacher to the school to teach
the children something different.

Sometimes the children like this, and sometimes they don't. This term they had a dancing teacher, Jiggling Jim.

Jiggling Jim taught them disco dancing, which Little Flo and Corkella thought was wonderful, while the two boys thought it was boring.

"I feel stupid," said Smudge.

"You are stupid, stupid," sniggered Ziggy, who was wearing a pair of joke vampire teeth so that he could scare everyone.

"Well, I love disco dancing," said Little Flo, leaping through the air like a pop star.

As for Corkella, she had just gone spinning overboard. SPLADDASH!

"Disco dancing is good for you!" roared Patagonia, who secretly dreamed of being a Disco Queen. "One day you will thank me for this."

"Fat chance," muttered Ziggy.

"I heard that!" roared Patagonia Clatterbottom. "No rice pudding for you tonight!"

"Don't like your piddly pudding anyhow," said Ziggy, and he bared his vampire teeth at her.

"Argh! You horrible child!"

2. Dick Lurkin's School

Not very far from Patagonia Clatterbottom's School for Pirates was a quite different kind of school.

It used to be a school for young highwaymen. Now it taught both girls and boys, so the name had been changed.

Dick Lurkin's School *for* Highwaypersons

Grrrrr!

This was where highwaymen (and women) sent their sons (and daughters) to learn how to be highwaymen (and women).

Dick Lurkin taught his pupils to ride and how to point a pistol properly. He also taught them how to wear a mask, look very fierce and say highwaymannish things like:

"Stand and deliver, your money or your liver! Grrrrr!"

Stand in the river, your mummy's got a shiver.

Stand and deliver, I'm in a dither.

Dick Lurkin said the "grrrrr!" at the end was the most important bit because it was scary.

They also learned how to make masks so that they could not be recognized.

When Dick thought his young pupils knew enough he would send them out to practise being highwaypersons.

They would jump out of the trees
and bushes, scare the pants off people
and then run off with them, giggling.

14

In other words they were a BIG NUISANCE. And if ever the School for Highwaypersons met the School for Pirates then there was an enormous fight, lots of noise and the highwaypersons always won. (This was because there were more of them and they all had big brothers.)

3. Presents for Patagonia

It was Patagonia Clatterbottom's birthday. She insisted that everyone give her a birthday present, and because it was her birthday she said that Jiggling Jim must dance with her.

"I've always wanted to be a Disco Queen," Patagonia sighed dreamily, waving her hanky.

"More like a Disco Dinosaur," Corkella muttered.

"I heard that!" screeched Patagonia, and she gave Jiggling Jim such a twirl that he went flying off and got stuck in the rigging.

"Leave him," ordered Patagonia.
"What have you children got for me?"

"It's a shell I found," said Little Flo.

"It's a picture I made," said Smudge.

"It's a sweet I saved," said Corkella.

"My present is special," said Ziggy.
"You have to sit down to get it."

She's a sooper-pooper!

Patagonia greedily rubbed her
hands and sat down.

SPLRRRRRRGH!!!

"It's a whoopee cushion!" cried
Mad Maggott. "I love whoopee
cushions."

"Throw that child overboard! He's a disgrace," bellowed Patagonia. But everyone was too busy laughing.

"We are going to have a party," she announced. "We need crisps and crackers, fizz and whizz and jelly and jam and jars of jollop. Snitty – to the shops!"

What a dreadful dee-doppa-doodah!

Off they all went, in a noisy, happy crowd – everyone except Jiggling Jim, who was still stuck in the rigging.

They went past the trees and bushes where the highwaypersons sometimes hid.

"Be careful," said Miss Fishgripp.

"Don't be scared," trembled Mad Maggott.

"Let's run," suggested Mrs Muggwump.

But the highwaypersons didn't jump out because the pirates didn't have anything worth stealing.

You can run, but you can't fly.

At the shop the pirates found everything they needed and they started back.

"Carry this," Patagonia told Little Flo. "And you carry this," she told Smudge. Soon everyone was loaded down with party food. (All except for Patagonia Clatterbottom, of course.) "This is going to be the best birthday bash ever," she said.

4. The Ambush

When they got to the trees and bushes – WHAT A SHOCK! Out jumped the highwaypersons (and their big brothers).

"Grrrrrrr!" growled Black Mask.

"Not yet, stupid. The 'Grrrr' goes at the end," hissed Monkey Mask.

"What do we say then?"

Spotty Mask stepped forward and waved a pistol in the air. "Stand and deliver, your mummy or your liver! Grrrrr!"

"We're highwaypersons and we are robbing you!" yelled Daisy Mask. "Hand over your mummies!"

"We heard you the first time," said Ziggy. "We haven't got our mummies with us."

"In that case we'll take all your shopping," said Monkey Mask.

"Oh no you won't. That's my birthday bash beanfeast," yelled Patagonia.

"Tough bananas!" Spotty Mask yelled back, and the highwaypersons leaped on to the pirates.

Biff! Baff! Boff!

When the dust cleared Patagonia's boat-pram was halfway up a tree, and so was Patagonia. The pirates were all

over the place, the party food had gone and so had a lot of their pants.

The pirates crawled back to the boat.

"Look at you!" cried Jiggling Jim, who had now escaped from the rigging. "Black eyes! Nosebleeds! Missing pants! What a mess!

"That's not the way to deal with highwaypersons. I shall teach you. Follow me."

"Another daft disco dance," groaned Ziggy. "This is all we need."

5. Secret Training

J iggling Jim surprised everyone
when he turned to Patagonia.
"Dearest Disco Queen,

you must learn too. You are my most beautiful dancer."

"Who? Me?" Patagonia turned the same colour as her knickers. (Flame red.)

Little Flo was astonished. "He needs his eyes testing," she whispered.

"I heard that," snapped the head teacher. "If Jiggling Jim says I am beautiful then I must be."

When the training was finished the young pirates seemed very pleased.

"I like that kind of dancing," said Ziggy, much to everyone's surprise.

Jiggling Jim smiled. "Now we must go and see those horrible highwaypeople and get back

the party food."

So off went the pirates again.
Patagonia and Jiggling Jim sang a
song as they danced down the road.

"A doo woppa diddle, and a bee
boppa boo, we're gonna make a mess
of the highway crew."

"What are they going on about?"
asked Smudge.

Then Jiggling Jim stopped so
suddenly that everyone bumped into
each other and they fell over
like a row of
dominoes.

Clinkety-clunkety-clonkety-clang!

"Ssssh! We're at the trees and
bushes," he hissed.

6. Battle Stations!

P atagonia climbed into the
boat-pram. "Oi!" she roared.
"You lily-livered load of land-lubbery

highway-hooligans! Give back our
food. If you don't we shall mash you
into . . ."

She broke off and hissed at her
pirates. "What shall we mash them
into?"

"Mash!" yelled the children.

"Exactly. We'll mash you into mash!" shouted Patagonia.

The trees and bushes rustled like mad and out jumped the highwaypersons.

"Sand in your liver, whatever the weather! Grrrrrrrrr!" cried Daisy Mask.

"Sam's all a quiver, his mummy's got a feather!" yelled Monkey Mask.

"You don't scare me!" announced Patagonia, and she fired her cannon.

Boom! The boat-pram shot backwards and the head teacher suddenly found herself upside

Yippeeeee!

down with her legs waving in the air. (Not a pretty sight!)

"Do that again!" taunted the highwaykids. "It was very funny."

Jiggling Jim turned to the pirates. "Remember our secret training," he said, with a wink. Then he called to the highwaypersons. "Let battle begin!"

7. More Biffing and Baffing

It was not long before the ground was littered with groaning highwaybodies. They had to hand

over all the food. The pirates tied
them up in a big bundle and stole
their pants.

Don't look!

"It's not fair!" cried the highwaypersons. "You wait until we tell Dick Lurkin. Then you'll be in trouble."

Ziggy towered over Monkey Mask. Suddenly he bared his vampire teeth.

"Eek!" squeaked Monkey Mask, and he fainted on the spot.

Patagonia Clatterbottom wrote a note and stuck it to the top of Spotty Mask's head.

Dear Dick Lurkin,
Never, ever, ever bother us again or my pirates will come and give your highwaymen (and women) another dancing lesson.

Love from
the Dazzling Disco Queen.
P.C.

"Dick Lurkin will never work out
who it's from," complained Ziggy.

"I heard that!" yelled Patagonia.

But since it was her birthday (and
because she was hungry for her
birthday tea), she decided to be nice
to everyone. The party began.

The pirates were halfway through
singing "Happy Birthday to You"
when there was a terrible noise and
trouble arrived.

8. The Birthday Bash

D ick Lurkin and all his highwaymen (and women, and their brothers and sisters) swarmed on to the deck of the pirate ship.

"Shiver me timbers!" cried
Patagonia. "Raaargh!"

"Throttle me fetlocks!" cried Dick.
"Grrrrrrr!"

Squeakle me
squawker!

"Why do they always talk rubbish?" asked everyone else.

But the highwaypersons hadn't come for a fight. They just wanted to join in the party.

Patagonia Clatterbottom wasn't too happy about this, but Little Flo and Smudge and all the other children thought it was brilliant.

"It's better with more of us," they pointed out.

They played loads of party games. They played "Pin the Eyepatch on the Pirate" and "Pass the Pistol", but the best game was "Musical Cannons". Everyone had to rush round the deck and when the music stopped they hid in a cannon. Ziggy fired one, accidentally on purpose, and Miss Fishgripp found herself far out at sea.

They had a disco too. Patagonia danced with Dick, who was very good at disco dancing. He even tossed Patagonia into the air, only to find himself holding her wooden leg, while Patagonia went flying up and up until she landed upside down in the crow's nest.

"It's the best birthday bash I've been to," said Corkella. She was dancing with Monkey Mask. Ziggy didn't think much of that and he showed his vampire teeth, but Monkey Mask had already seen them so he didn't care.

"I like you," he told Corkella. "Can I give you a kiss?"

"I heard that!" roared Patagonia
Clatterbottom from the crow's nest.
"No kissing. Pirates do NOT do
kissing!"

"Just ignore her," smiled Corkella.

Daisy Mask stood shyly next to
Ziggy. "I'd like to kiss you," she said.

"Stop that at once!" bellowed
Patagonia. "And as for you, Dick
Lurkin, you give me my leg back, you
light-fingered leg-lifter.

"Come back here at once!"